The Hare and the Tortoise

and other stories

Miles
Kelly

First published in 2011 by Miles Kelly Publishing Ltd
Harding's Barn, Bardfield End Green, Thaxted, Essex, CM6 3PX, UK

This edition printed 2013

2 4 6 8 10 9 7 5 3

Publishing Director Belinda Gallagher

Creative Director Jo Cowan

Editor Amanda Askew

Senior Designer Joe Jones

Designer Kayleigh Allen

Production Manager Elizabeth Collins

Reprographics Anthony Cambray, Stephan Davis, Jennifer Hunt

Assets Lorraine King

ISBN 978-1-84810-442-6

Printed in China

British Library Cataloguing-in-Publication Data
A catalogue record for this book is available from the British Library

ACKNOWLEDGEMENTS
Artworks are from the Miles Kelly Artwork Bank

Made with paper from a sustainable forest

www.mileskelly.net
info@mileskelly.net
www.factsforprojects.com

Contents

Chicken Licken

An English folk tale

One fine day Chicken Licken went for a walk in the woods. Now Chicken Licken was not very bright, and he was also rather inclined to act first and think after. So when an acorn fell on his head, he decided immediately that the sky must be falling in. He set off as fast as he could to tell the king. On the way he met Henny Penny and Cocky Locky.

"I am off to tell the king that the sky is falling

in," he clucked importantly.

"We will come too," said Henny Penny and Cocky Locky.

So Chicken Licken, Henny Penny and Cocky Locky set off to find the King. On the way they met Ducky Lucky and Drakey Lakey.

"We are off to tell the king that the sky is falling in," clucked Chicken Licken importantly.

"We will come too," said Ducky Lucky and Drakey Lakey.

So Chicken Licken, Henny Penny, Cocky Locky, Ducky Lucky and Drakey Lakey all set off to find the king. On the way they met Goosey Loosey and Turkey Lurkey.

"We are off to tell the king that the sky is falling in," clucked Chicken Licken importantly.

"We will come too," said Goosey Loosey and Turkey Lurkey.

So Chicken Licken, Henny Penny, Cocky Locky, Ducky Lucky, Drakey Lakey, Goosey Loosey and Turkey Lurkey all set off to find the king. On the way they met Foxy Loxy.

"We are off to tell the king that the sky is falling in," clucked Chicken Licken importantly.

"What a good thing I met you all," said Foxy Loxy with a cunning smile. "I know the way, follow me."

Chicken Licken

So Chicken Licken, Henny Penny, Cocky Locky, Ducky Lucky, Drakey Lakey, Goosey Loosey and Turkey Lurkey all set off behind Foxy Loxy. He led them all straight to his den where he ate every single one of them for his dinner! So the king never heard that the sky was falling in (it didn't, of course).

The Three Little Pigs

An English folk tale

There once was a mother pig who had three little pigs. They were very poor indeed, and the day came when the mother pig could no longer look after the family. She sent the three little pigs out into the big, wide world to seek their fortunes.

The first little pig met a man carrying a big bundle of straw.

"Oh, please may I have that bundle of straw to build myself a house?" asked the first little pig.

The man was tired of carrying the bundle of straw so he gladly gave it to the first little pig.

The first little pig built a very fine house out of the bundle of straw, and he lived there very happily. Then along came a big bad wolf.

"Little pig, little pig, let me in!" shouted the wolf.

"No, no, not by the hair on my chinny chin chin. I'll not let you in," squeaked the first little pig.

"Then I'll huff and I'll puff, and I'll blow your house down," yelled the wolf. And he did. He huffed and he puffed and he blew the straw house down. The first little pig ran away as fast as his trotters would carry him.

Now the second little pig met a man carrying a bundle of sticks.

"Oh, please may I have that bundle

of sticks to build myself a house?" asked the second little pig. The man was tired of carrying the bundle of sticks so he gladly gave it to the second little pig.

The second little pig built a very fine house out of the sticks, and he lived there very happily. Then along came the big bad wolf.

"Little pig, little pig, let me in!" shouted the wolf.

"No, no, not by the hair on my chinny chin chin. I'll not let you in," squeaked the second little pig.

"Then I'll huff and I'll puff, and I'll blow your house down," yelled the wolf. And he did. He huffed and he puffed and he blew the stick house down. The second little pig ran away as fast as his trotters would carry him.

Now the third little pig met a man carrying a big load of bricks.

"Oh, please may I have that load of bricks to build myself a house?" asked the third little pig. The man was very tired from carrying the big load of bricks so he gave it to the third little pig.

The third little pig built a very fine house out of the bricks, and he lived there very happily. Then along came the big bad wolf.

"Little pig, little pig, let me in!" shouted the wolf.

"No, no, not by the hair on my chinny chin chin. I'll not let you in," squeaked the third little pig.

"Then I'll huff and I'll puff, and I'll blow your house down," yelled the wolf. And he tried. He huffed and he puffed but he could not blow the brick house down.

"Little pig, little pig, I am coming down your chimney to get you," bellowed the wolf.

"Please yourself," called the third little pig who was busy with some preparations of his own.

"Little pig, little pig, I have my front paws down your chimney," threatened the wolf.

"Please yourself," called the third little pig who was still busy with some preparations of his own.

"Little pig, little pig, I have my great bushy tail down your chimney," called the wolf.

"Please yourself," called the third little pig who was now sitting in his rocking chair by the fireside.

"Little pig, little pig, here I come!" and with a great rush and a huge SPLOSH! the big bad wolf fell right into the big pot of boiling water that the clever little pig had placed on the fire, right under the chimney. The wolf scrabbled and splashed and scrambled out of the big pot and ran as fast as ever he could right out of the front door. And he was never seen again. The third little pig managed to find his two brothers, and they went and fetched their mother. And they are all still living happily together in the little brick house.

The Hare and the Tortoise

An Aesop's fable

The day that Tortoise challenged Hare to a race, all the animals laughed so hard that their tummies ached. But Tortoise was fed-up with Hare whizzing round him all the time, teasing him about how slow he was. 'I'll show that Hare, if it's the last thing I do!' Tortoise promised himself.

Hare thought that Tortoise's little joke was extremely funny. For that's all Hare thought it was – a joke. Hare never expected that Tortoise would actually go through with his mad idea. So his eyes nearly popped out of his head when he arrived at the starting line to see Tortoise already there, limbering up in a slow, stiff, creaky sort of way.

"Be careful there, old chap!" Hare worried, as he realized his friend was serious.

"You don't want to do yourself an injury."

"Don't worry about me," replied Tortoise. "You should be working out how you're going to beat me. Ha! You won't see me for dust!"

A huge crowd of animals had gathered to watch the race and they all cheered and clapped and jumped up and down at Tortoise's bold remark.

Suddenly, Hare started to feel rather annoyed. "All right then. If that's the way you want it!" he snapped. "I was going to give you a headstart, but obviously you won't be wanting one."

"No need," breezed Tortoise, although his little heart was pumping inside his shell. "First one to the windmill's the winner."

Hare peered into the distance. The windmill was three fields away. He could get there in less than a minute without losing his breath. But surely it would take Tortoise all day to reach it!

"Three! Twit-Two! One!" cried Barn Owl, and Tortoise lifted one leg over the starting line amid thunderous applause.

The stunned Hare watched in amazement as Tortoise began to crawl slowly away. Well, you have to hand it to Tortoise! Hare thought, seeing the funny side of things again. He's certainly got a good sense of humour and a lot of guts!

Hare sat down next to the starting line under a shady tree. It was a beautiful sunny day and it was very pleasant to sit there in the dappled light, watching Tortoise amble peacefully into the field. Hare's eyes shut and his head drooped before he even realized he was sleepy...

Meanwhile, Tortoise was remembering what his mum had told him as a child: Slow and steady does it, son. Slow and steady does it. And Tortoise kept on going and didn't give up.

Hare didn't wake up until the night air was so cold that it was freezing his whiskers. Where am I? he thought. And then suddenly he remembered the race. Hare leapt to his feet and squinted into the moonlight, but there was no sign of Tortoise. All at once, he heard a faint sound of cheering coming from a long way off, and he saw tiny dark figures jumping up and down around the windmill. "Surely not!" Hare gasped, and shot off over the fields like an arrow. He arrived at the windmill just in time to *see* all the animals hoisting Tortoise – the champion – on their shoulders. And of course, after that, Hare never ever teased his friend about being slow again.

Little Red Riding Hood

An English folk tale

There was once a little girl who lived in the middle of a deep, dark forest with her mother and father, who was a woodcutter. The little girl always wore a red cloak with a hood, and so she was called Little Red Riding Hood.

One day she decided to visit her granny who lived some way from the woodcutter's cottage. She took a basket with a cake her mother had baked and set off. Now the last thing her mother had said to Little Red Riding Hood was, "Don't leave the path, and don't talk to any strangers." But Little Red Riding Hood was not really listening. So when she saw some bluebells growing under a tree, she left the path and began to pick a bunch for her granny. Slowly, slowly she wandered further away from the path, deeper into the trees. Suddenly, she was not alone. There in front of her stood a great big wolf. Now Little Red Riding Hood had not met a wolf before so she did not realize that wolves are not the kind of animals to be too friendly with.

"Good day, little girl," said the wolf with a snarly sort of a smile. "What is your name and where are you going?"

"My name is Little Red Riding Hood. I am going to visit my granny, and I am taking her a cake to eat," replied Little Red Riding Hood.

The wolf was delighted. Not only a little girl to eat but a granny AND a cake as well!

"And where does your granny live, little girl?" asked the wolf, trying hard to smile nicely despite his fierce teeth.

Little Red Riding Hood told the wolf where her granny lived, and went on picking bluebells. The wolf slipped away through the trees and soon found the granny's cottage. He tapped on the door and said, in a disguised voice, "Hello, granny. It is Little Red Riding Hood. I have brought you a cake, will you let me in?"

As soon as the door was open, the wolf bounded in and gobbled the granny all up! He put on her nightcap and shawl and climbed into her bed. Soon he heard Little Red Riding Hood coming and he tried his snarly smile again.

"Hello, granny," said Little Red Riding Hood. "I have brought you a cake and these bluebells," and she came up to the bedside.

"Goodness, granny! What great big eyes you have!" she said.

"All the better to see you with," growled the wolf.

Little Red Riding Hood could not help noticing the wolf's teeth.

"Goodness, granny! What great big teeth you have!"

"All the better to eat you with!" snapped the wolf and gobbled up Little Red Riding Hood. He gobbled up the cake in the basket as well and then, very full indeed, he fell fast asleep, snoring loudly.

Now by great good luck, Little Red

Little Red Riding Hood

Riding Hood's father was passing by the cottage, and when he heard the terrible snores, he put his head round the door to see who was making such a noise. He was horrified to see the wolf so he took his axe and made a great slit down the wolf's tummy. Out jumped Little Red Riding Hood and granny. She stitched up the wolf's tummy and told him to mind his manners in future. Then, as there was no cake left for tea, they all went back home, and Little Red Riding Hood's mother made pancakes. I am pleased to say Little Red Riding Hood had learnt her lesson, and she never spoke to wolves again.

Goldilocks and the Three Bears

By Andrew Lang

Once upon a time there was a little girl called Goldilocks who lived in a great forest with her mother and her father. Now ever since she was tiny, her mother had told her she must never, ever wander off into the forest for it was full of wild creatures, especially bears. But as Goldilocks grew older she longed to explore the forest.

One washday, when her mother was busy in the kitchen, hidden in clouds of steam, Goldilocks sneaked off down the path that led deep into the forest. At first she was happy, looking at the wild flowers and listening to the birds singing, but it did not take long for her to become hopelessly lost.

She wandered for hours and hours and, as it

grew darker, she became frightened. She started to cry, but then she saw a light shining through the trees. She rushed forward, sure she had found her way home, only to realize that it was not her own cottage that she was looking at. Even so, she opened the door and looked inside.

On a scrubbed wooden table there were three bowls of steaming hot porridge – a big one, a middle-sized one and a little one. Goldilocks was so tired that she quite forgot all her manners and just sat down at the table. The big bowl was too tall for her to reach. The middle-sized bowl was too hot. But the little one was just right, so she ate all the porridge.

By the warm fire there were three chairs – a big one, a middle-sized one and a little one. Goldilocks couldn't climb up into the big one. The middle-sized one was too hard. The little one was just the right size, but as soon as she sat down, it broke into pieces. Goldilocks scrambled to her feet and then noticed there were steps going upstairs, where she found three beds – a big one, a middle-sized one and a little one. The big bed was too hard. The middle-sized one was too soft. But the little one was just right and she was soon fast asleep.

The cottage belonged to three bears, and it was not long before they came home. They knew at once that someone had been inside.

Father Bear growled, "Who has been eating my porridge?"

Mother Bear grumbled, "Who has been eating my porridge?"

And Baby Bear gasped, "Who has been eating my porridge, AND has eaten it all?"

The bears looked round the room. They looked at the chairs by the warm fire.

Father Bear growled, "Who has been sitting in my chair?"

Goldilocks and the Three Bears

Mother Bear grumbled, "Who has been sitting in my chair?" And Baby Bear gasped, "Who has been sitting in my chair, AND has broken it to bits?"

The bears went upstairs to look at their beds.

Father Bear growled, "Who has been sleeping in my bed?"

Mother Bear grumbled, "Who has been sleeping in my bed?"

And Baby Bear gasped, "Who has been sleeping in my bed, AND is still there?"

Suddenly Goldilocks woke up. All she could see was three very cross-looking bears. She jumped off the bed, ran down the stairs and out of the door. She ran and ran and ran, and by good fortune found herself outside her own cottage. Her mother and father scolded her, but then gave her lots of hugs and kisses, and a big bowl of soup. Goldilocks had certainly learnt her lesson, and she never ever wandered off again.

The Gingerbread Man

An English folk tale

One fine sunny day, an old woman was making some ginger biscuits. She had a little dough left over and so she made a gingerbread man for her husband. She gave him raisins for eyes and cherries for buttons, and put a smile on his face with a piece of orange peel. Then she popped the biscuits and gingerbread man in the oven. A little while later, she lifted the tray out of the oven when the biscuits were cooked. Suddenly, the gingerbread man hopped off the tray and ran straight out of the door! The old woman ran after him, and her husband ran after her, but they couldn't catch the gingerbread man. He called out, "Run, run, as fast as you can! You can't catch me, I'm the gingerbread man!"

The Gingerbread Man

The old dog in his kennel ran after the old man and the old woman, but he couldn't catch the gingerbread man. The ginger cat, who had been asleep in the sun, ran after the dog, but she couldn't catch the gingerbread man. He called out, "Run, run, as fast as you can! You can't catch me, I'm the gingerbread man!"

The brown cow in the meadow lumbered after the cat, but she couldn't catch the gingerbread man.

The black horse in the stable galloped after the cow but he couldn't catch the gingerbread man. He called out, "Run, run, as fast as you can! You can't catch me, I'm the gingerbread man!"

The fat pink pig in the sty trotted after the horse, but she couldn't catch the gingerbread man. The rooster flapped and squawked after the pig but he couldn't catch the gingerbread man. He called out, "Run, run, as fast as you can! You can't catch me, I'm the gingerbread man!"

He ran and ran, and the old woman and the old man, the dog and the cat, the cow and the horse, the pig and the rooster all ran after him. He kept running until he came to the river. For the first time since he had hopped out of the oven, the gingerbread man had to stop running.

The Gingerbread Man

"Help, help! How can I cross the river?" he cried.
A sly fox suddenly appeared by his side.

"I could carry you across the river," said the sly fox.

The gingerbread man jumped onto the fox's back, and the fox slid into the water.

"My feet are getting wet," complained the gingerbread man.

"Well, jump onto my head," smiled the fox, showing a lot of very sharp teeth. And he kept on swimming.

"My feet are still getting wet," complained the gingerbread man again after a while.

"Well, jump onto my nose," smiled the fox, showing even more very sharp teeth.

The gingerbread man jumped onto the fox's nose, and SNAP! the fox gobbled him all up. When the fox climbed out of the river on the other side, all that was left of the naughty gingerbread man was a few crumbs. So the old woman and the old man, the dog and the cat, the cow and the horse, the pig and the rooster all went home and shared the ginger biscuits. They were delicious.